The Night Is Singing

by Jacqueline Davies

illustrated by Kyrsten Brooker

DIAL BOOKS FOR YOUNG READERS

DIAL BOOKS FOR YOUNG READERS • A division of Penguin Young Readers Group • Published by The Penguin Group • Penguin Group (USA) Inc., 375 Hudson Street, New York, NY 10014, U.S.A. • Penguin Group (Canada), 90 Eglinton Avenue East, Suite 700, Toronto, Ontario, Canada M4P 2Y3 (a division of Pearson Penguin Canada Inc.) • Penguin Books Ltd, 80 Strand, London WC2R 0RL, England • Penguin Ireland, 25 St. Stephen's Green, Dublin 2, Ireland (a division of Penguin Books Ltd.) • Penguin Group (Australia), Camberwell Road, Camberwell, Victoria 3124, Australia (a division of Pearson Australia Group Pty Ltd) • Penguin Books India Pvt Ltd, 11 Community Centre, Panchsheel Park, New Delhi - 110 017, India • Penguin Group (NZ), Cnr Airborne and Rosedale Roads, Albany, Auckland, New Zealand (a division of Pearson New Zealand Ltd) Penguin Books (South Africa) (Pty) Ltd, 24 Sturdee Avenue, Rosebank, Johannesburg 2196, South Africa Penguin Books Ltd, Registered Offices: 80 Strand, London WC2R 0RL, England

Library of Congress Cataloging-in-Publication Data Davies, Jacqueline, date. • The night is singing / by Jacqueline Davies ; illustrated by Kyrsten Brooker p. cm. • Summary: Rhyming text tells of lullabies that can be heard in the sounds of the night, such as a radiator's hiss, a cat's shadowboxing, and a rainstorm's drumming. • ISBN 0-8037-3004-7 • [1. Night—Fiction. 2. Sound—Fiction. 3. Lullabies—Fiction. 4. Stories in rhyme.] I. Brooker, Kyrsten, ill. II. Title. PZ8.3.D27Ni 2006 • [E]—dc22 • 2004014161

The art was created using collage and oil paint on gessoed watercolor paper.

For Sam, Henry, and Mae, who never minded my lullabies,
even though I sing off-key
~J.D.

For Kieran
~K.B.

When the night is gently falling,
And the moon is on the rise,
Close your eyes,
Close your eyes . . .

The night is singing lullabies.

Hear the hissing,
Soft as kissing,
From the radiator grate.
Hear the chiming
Tell-the-timing
Of the hall clock striking eight.

Up you go.
Tippy-toe.

The house is singing lullabies.

Night-flight squalling,
Gray geese calling,
Streak-and-fly across the sky.
Noisy crying,
Shadows flying,
Leaving town, they shout *good-bye*.

Watch them go.
Sleepy? No!

The sky is singing lullabies.

Tabby leaping,
No more sleeping,
Shadowboxing with your nose.
Romp and tumble,
Kitty rumble,
Flying paws and tickled toes.

Back in bed.
Kiss his head.

Your cat is singing lullabies.

Pip-pip-popping,
Acorns dropping,
On the roof above your head.
Branches creaking,
Almost speaking,
Wish you knew what they just said?

No mistake.
Still awake.

The trees are singing lullabies.

Wind a'blowing,
Come-and-going,
Playing tag beneath the eaves.
Tree limbs tussling,
Hear the rustling
Of the falling, brawling leaves.

Breezy tree—
Can't get me!

The wind is singing lullabies.

Hear the drumming,
Storm is coming,
As a shutter comes undone.
Thunder bolting,
Lightning jolting,
Now the rainstorm has begun.

Something crashing,
Tree limbs lashing,
As the heavens open wide.
Hear the raindrops,
Hit-the-pane drops,
You are glad to be inside.

Tip-tap beat.
Mama's feet?

Rain is slowing,
Soft wind blowing,
As the storm clouds scud away.
You are safe, dear.
You are loved here,
In this house at end of day.

Kiss and hug.
Curled up snug

While Mama sings you lullabies.

Now the moon beams down upon you,
And the stars ignite the skies.
'Til you rise,
'Til you rise,

The night will sing you lullabies,

The night will sing you lullabies.

Shhh. Shhh. Shhh.